THE FIRST THOUSAND WORDS IN RUSSIAN

With Easy Pronunciation Guide

Heather Amery and Katrina Kirilenko

Illustrated by Stephen Cartwright

Pronunciation Guide by Lindsay Alexeiev

дома
doma

ванная
vannaya

гостиная
gasteenaya

ванна
vanna

мыло
myla

кран
kran

мыльные пузыри
mylny-ye poozyry

зубная щётка
zoobnaya shchyotka

вода
vada

полотенце
palatyentsye

губка
goobka

душ
doosh

зубная паста
zoobnaya pasta

умывальная раковина
oomyvalnaya rakoveena

унитаз
ooneetaz

книжный шкаф
kneezhny shkaf

стол
stol

радио
radeeo

батарея отопления
bataryeya ataplyeneeye

шерсть
sherst

обои
aboy

часы
chasy

ковёр
kavyor

подушка
padooshka

проигрыватель
pra-eegry vatyel

4

спальня
spalnaya

прихожая
preekhozhaya

лампа
lampa

постель
pastyel

комод
komod

щётка
shchyotka

подушка
padooshka

шкаф
shkaf

коврик
kovreek

картины
karteeny

пуховое одеяло
pookhavaye adyeala

одежда
adyezhda

расчёска
raschyoska

зеркало
zyerkalo

простыня
prastynya

лестница
lyestneetsa

паук
paook

кресло
kryeslo

письма
peesma

телефон
tyelyefon

паутина
paooteena

муха
mookha

газета
gazsyeta

вешалка
vyeshalka

5

КУХНЯ
kookhnya

холодильник
khaladeelneek

стаканы
stakany

часы
chasy

ложки
lozhkee

передник
pyeryedneek

розетка
razyetka

кастрюли
kastryoolee

блюдца
blyoodtsye

утюг
ootyoog

чайник
chayneek

швабра
shvabra

пылесос
pylyesos

6

раковина
rakoveena

вилки
veelkee

дверь
dvyer

пыльная тряпка
pylnaya tryapka

табуретка
tabooryetka

ножи
nozhee

лоск
losk

плита
pleeta

кафельная плитка
kafyelnaya pleetka

ящик
yashcheek

мусор
moosar

сковорода
skavarada

стиральная машина
steeralnaya masheena

совок для мусора
savok dlya moosara

тарелки
taryelkee

гладильная доска
gladeenaya daska

стиральный порошок
steeralny parashok

щётка
shchyotka

шкаф
shkaf

стол
stol

лампа
lampa

чашки
chashkee

чайные ложки
chayny-ye lozhkee

спички
speechkee

ключ
klyooch

щётка
shchyetka

миски
meeskee

7

тачка
tachka

улей
oolyey

улитка
ooleetka

кирпичи
keerpeechee

мусорный ящик
moosarny yashcheek

гусеница
goosyeneetsa

лопата
lapata

муравей
mooravyey

голубь
galoob

сточный жёлоб
stochny zhyolab

лестница
lyestneetsa

семена
syemyena

8 **сарай**
saray

сад
sad

червяк
chyervyak

цветы
tsvyety

разбрызгиватель
razbrysgeevatyel

кость
kost

живая изгородь
zheevaya eezgarad

кельма
kyelma

газонокосилка
gazanaseelka

тропинка
trapeenka

дерево
dyeryeva

вилы
veely

листья
leestya

щётка
shchyetka

шланг
shlang

мотыга
matyga

дым
dym

пчёла
pchyola

грабли
grablee

теплица
tyepleetsa

детская коляска
dyetskaya kalyaska

оса
asa

трава
trava

рассада
rassada

костёр
kastyor

птичье гнездо
pteechye gnyezdo

палки
palkee

мастерская
mastyerskaya

наждачная бумага
nazhdachnaya boomaga

дрель
dryel

болты
bolty

гвоздик с широкой шляпкой
gvozdeek s sheerokay shlyapkay

пила
peela

опилки
apeelkee

молоток
malatok

напильник
napeelneek

ящик для инструментов
yashcheek dlya eenstroomyentov

отвёртка
atvyortka

доска
daska

банка с краской
banka s krackay

стружки
stroozhkee

перочинный ножик
pyeracheenny nozheek

10

бочка
bochka

топор
tapor

гайки
gaykee

рулетка
roolyetka

шурупы
shooroopy

лестница
lyestneetsa

гвозди
gvozdee

тиски
teeskee

дрова
drava

верстак
vyerstak

банки
bankee

деревянный брусок
dyeryevyanny broosok

рубанок
roobanak

11

гараж
garazh

скорая помощь
skoraya pomashch

велосипед
vyelaseepyed

яма
yama

кафе
kafye

тротуар
tratooar

магазин
magazeen

светофор
svyetafor

труба
trooba

грузовик
groozaveek

переход
pyeryekhod

ступеньки
stoopyenkee

мужчина
moozhcheena

улица
ooleetsa

гостиница
gasteeneetsa

милицейская
машина
meeleetsyeyskaya masheena

каток
katok

отбойный
молоток
atboyny malatok

школа
shkola

площадка для игр
plashchadka dlya eegr

жилой дом
zheeloy dom

12

памятник
pamyatneek

автобус
avtoboos

такси
taksee

прицеп
preetsyep

трубы
trooby

крыша
krysha

рынок
rynak

фабрика
fabreeka

антенна
antyena

фургон
foorgon

милиционер
meeleetsyanyer

пожарная машина
pazharnaya masheena

дом
dom

женщина
zhyenshcheena

экскаватор
ekskavator

церковь
tsyerkov

кинотеатр
keenatyeatr

машина
masheena

мотоцикл
matatseekl

водитель
vadeetyel

фонарный столб
fanarny stolb

13

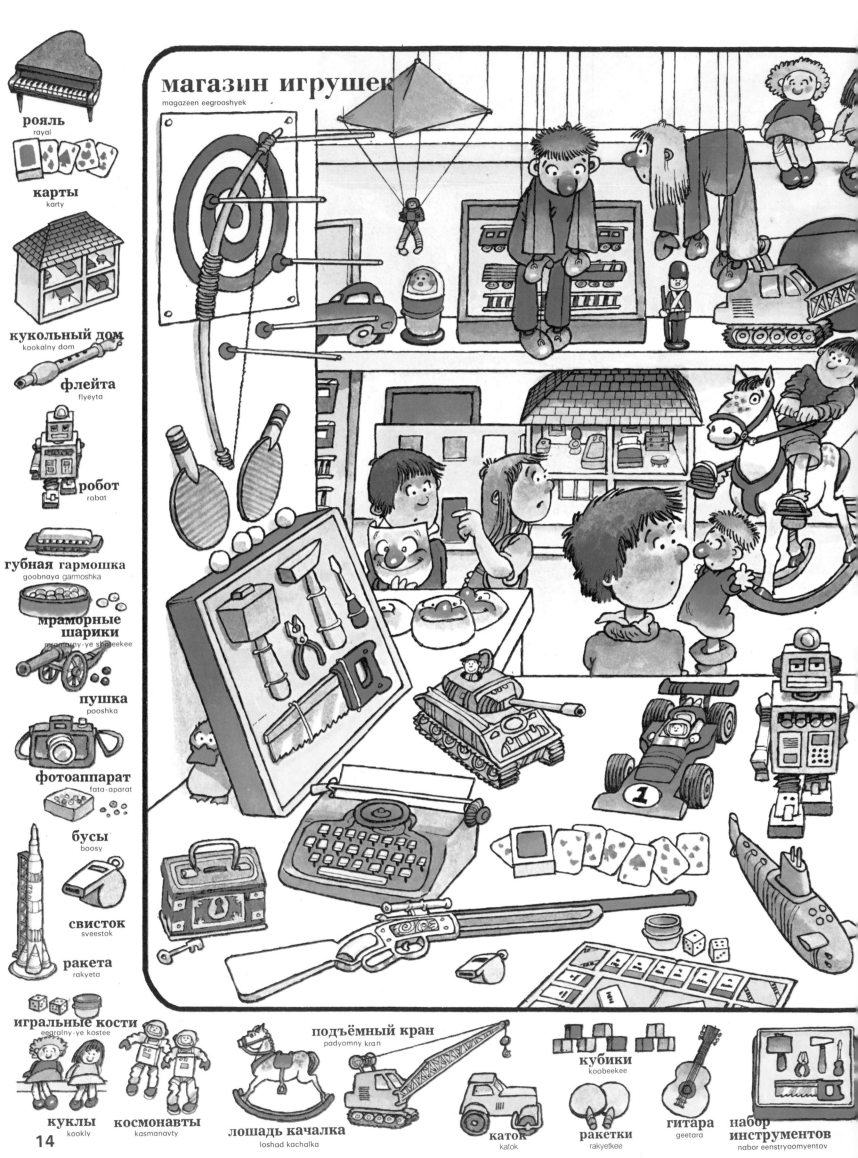

магазин игрушек
magazeen eegrooshyek

рояль
rayal

карты
karty

кукольный дом
kookalny dom

флейта
flyeyta

робот
robat

губная гармошка
goobnaya garmoshka

мраморные шарики
mramorny-ye shareekee

пушка
pooshka

фотоаппарат
fata-aparat

бусы
boosy

свисток
sveestok

ракета
rakyeta

игральные кости
eegralny-ye kostee

куклы
kookly

космонавты
kasmanavty

лошадь качалка
loshad kachalka

подъёмный кран
padyomny kran

каток
katok

кубики
koobeekee

ракетки
rakyetkee

гитара
geetara

набор инструментов
nabor eenstryoomyentov

14

удилище
oodeeleeshchye

краски
kraskee

пластилин
plasteeleen

парашют
parashyoot

пишущая машинка
peeshooshchaya masheena

яхта
yakhta

мишень
meeshyen

танк
tank

солдатики
saldateekee

замок
zamak

копилка
kapeelka

железная дорога
zhyelyeznaya daroga

барабаны
barabany

мячи
myachee

марионетки
mareeanyetkee

гоночная машина
ganochnaya masheena

маски
maskee

труба
trooba

лук и стрела
look ee stryela

ружьё
roozhyo

подводная лодка
padvodnaya lodka

15

мяч
myach

шнур
shnoor

обед в походе
abyed b pakhodye

пикник
peekneek

**воздуш–
ный
змей**
vazdooshny zmyey

мороженое
marozhyenaye

собака
sabaka

качели
kachyelee

калитка
kaleetka

тропинка
trapeenka

головастики
galavasteekee

16

горка для катания
gorka dlya kataneeya

парк
park

лягушка
lyagooshka

куст
koost

ролики
roleekee

дети
dyetee

самокат
samakat

лебеди
lyebyedee

ребёнок
ryebyonak

земля
zyemlya

забор
zabor

детская dyetskaya
складная skladnaya
коляска kalyaska

птицы
pteetsy

детские качели
dyetskeeye kachyelee

цветы
tsvyety

лужа
loozha

утята
ootyata

скакалка
skakalka

яхта
yakhta

клумба
kloomba

скамейка
skamyeyka

озеро
ozyera

поводок
pavodak

утка
ootka

деревья
dyeryevya

17

зоопарк
za-apark

панда
panda

летучая мышь
lyetoochaya mysh

пингвин
peengveen

гиппопотам
geepapatam

крыло
krylo

лапы
lapy

орёл
aryol

кенгуру
kyengooroo

перья
pyerya

страус
straoos

волк
volk

обезьяна
abyazyana

пеликан
pyeleekan

жираф
zheeraf

горилла
gareella

медведь
myedvyed

лев
lyev

бобр
bobr

львята
lvyata

крокодил
krakadeel

18

рога
raga

олень
alyen

верблюд
vyerblyood

тюлень
tyoolyen

обезьяны
abyesyany

белый медведь
byely myedvyed

хобот
khabot

зебра
zyebra

слон
slon

хвост
khvost

буйвол
boovyel

акула
akoola

носорог
nasarog

козёл
kazyol

дельфин
dyelfeen

леопард
lyeapard

кит
keet

тигр
teegr

рельсы
ryelsy

кондуктор
kandooktar

локомотив
lakamateev

буфера
boofyera

вагон-ресторан
vagon-ryestoran

вагоны
vagony

машинист
masheeneest

товарный поезд
tavarny poyezd

платформа
platforma

семафор
syemafor

проводник
pravodneek

чемоданы
chyemadany

фара
fara

вокзал
vakzal

гараж
garazh

мотор
mator

маслёнка
maslyonka

аккумулятор
akoomoolyatar

бензовоз
byenzavoz

20

аэропорт
a-eraport

стюардесса
styooardyessa

вертолёт
vyertalyot

взлётнопоса-
дочная полоса
vzlyotnapasadachnaya palosa

самолёт
samalyot

наблюдательная
башня
nablyoodatyelnaya bashnya

пилот
peelot

мойка машин
moyka masheen

багажник
bagazhneek

насос
nasos

бензоколонка
byenzakalonka

колесо
kalyeso

гаечный ключ
gayechny klyooch

шина
sheena

капот
kapot

аварийная машина
avareenaya masheena

масло
masla

21

ветряная мельница
vyetryanaya myelneetsa

лес
lyes

сарай
saray

кролики
kroleekee

мотылёк
matylyok

лиса
leesa

речка
ryechka

указатель
ookazatyel

цветы
tsvyety

белка
byelka

бабочка
babachka

птицы
pteetsy

барсук
barsook

деревня
dyeryevnya

холм
kholm

лисята
leesyata

туннель
toonnyel

деревня
dyeryevnya

сова
sava

22

воздушный шар
vazdooshny shar

автофургон
avtafoorgon

поленья
palyenya

палатки
palatkee

дорога
daroga

мост
most

баржа
barzha

водопад
vadapad

горы
gory

камни
kamnee

крот
krot

шлюз
shlyooz

рыбак
rybak

камни
kamnee

канал
kanal

поезд
poyezd

река
ryeka

23

ферма
fyerma

пруд
prood

овцы
ovtsy

стог сена
stog syena

утки
ootkee

прицеп
preetsyep

ягнята
yagnyata

забор
zabor

чердак
chyerdak

свинарник
sveenarneek

бык
byk

грязь
gryaz

поросята
parasyata

амбар
ambar

хлев
khlyev

фермер
fyermyer

повозка
pavozka

пони
ponee

трактор
traktor

седло
syedla

гуси
goosee

брикет
breekyet

мешки
myeshkee

24

грузовик
groozaveek

фруктовый сад
frooktovy sad

курятник
kooryatneek

коровник
karovneek

корова
karova

утята
ootyata

петух
pyetookh

телёнок
tyelyonok

плуг
ploog

пастух
pastookh

овчарка
avcharka

индюки
eendyookee

пугало
poogala

жилой дом на ферме
zheeloy dom na fyermye

куры
koory

цыплята
tsyplyata

свиньи
sveenee

лошадь
loshad

гусята
goosta

поле
polye

сено
syeno

зерно
zyerno

у моря
oo morya

парусная лодка
paroosnaya lodka

море
morye

весло
vyeslo

маяк
mayak

лопатка
lapatka

ведро
vyedro

морская звезда
morskaya zvyezda

песчаный замок
pyeschany zamok

чайка
chayka

флаг
flag

краб
krab

моряк
maryak

соломеная шляпа
salomyenaya shlyapa

бакен
bakyen

остров
ostrav

гавань
gavan

шезлонг
shyezlong

моторная лодка
matornaya lodka

водно-лыжник
vodna-lyzhneek

26

волны
volny

морская
раковина
morskaya rakaveena

утёс
ootyos

корабль
karabl

байдарка
baydarka

галька
galka

мяч
myach

скалы
skaly

ласты
lasty

морская
водоросль
morskaya vadareel

сеть
syet

весло
vyeslo

рыбачья лодка
rybachya lodka

зонт
zont

осёл
asyol

танкер
tankyer

гребная лодка
gryebnaya lodka

купальный
костюм
koopalny kastyoom

верёвка
vyeryovka

27

в школе
v shkolya

аквариум
akvareeoooom

значок
znachok

потолок
patalok

карандаши
karandashee

мальчики
malcheekee

календарь
kalyendar

стена
styena

корзина для бумаг
karzeena dlya boomag

ножницы
nozhneetsy

4+2 =
3-2 =

арифметические задачи
areefmyeteecheskeeye zadachee

линейка
leenyeyka

парта
parta

28 **фотографии**
fatagrafee

краски
kraskee

бумага
boomaga

кисти
keestee

колокольчик
kalakolcheek

абвгдеёжз
ийклмнопр
стуфхцчшш
ъыьэюя

алфавит
alfaveet

коробки
karobkee

книги
kneegee

а б в г д е ё ж з
и й к л м н о п р
с т у ф х ц ч ш щ
ъ ы ь э ю я

рисунок
reesoonak

ручки
roochkee

мел
myel

мольберт
molbyert

пол
pol

растения
rasteeneeya

девочки
dyevachkee

глобус
globoos

клей
klyey

ручка
roochka

блокнот
blaknot

канцелярская кнопка
kantsyelyarskaya knopka

рисунок
reesoonak

карта
karta

цветной мелок
tsvyetnoy myelok

лампа
lampa

жалюзи
zhalyoozee

доска
daska

резинка
ryezeenka

учительница
oocheetyelneetsa

29

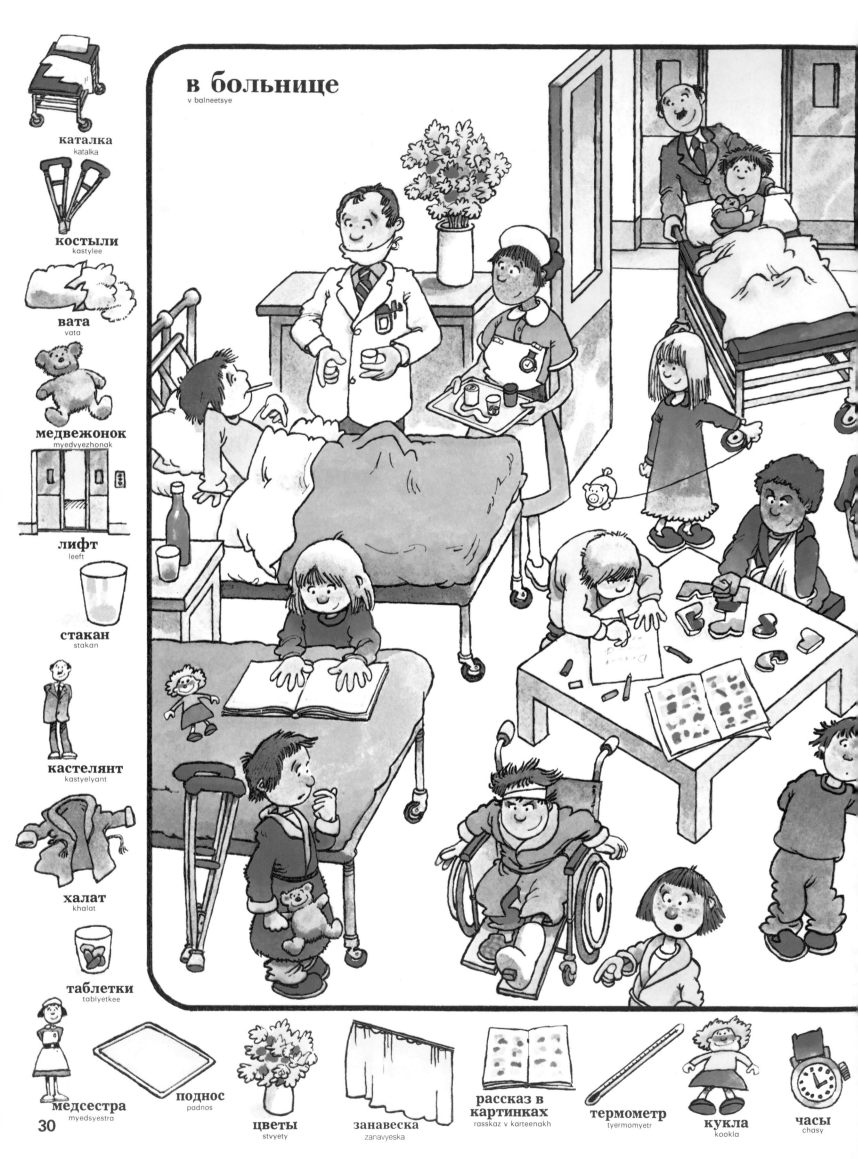

в больнице
v balneetsye

каталка
katalka

костыли
kastylee

вата
vata

медвежонок
myedvyezhonak

лифт
leeft

стакан
stakan

кастелянт
kastyelyant

халат
khalat

таблетки
tablyetkee

медсестра
myedsyestra

поднос
padnos

цветы
stvyety

занавеска
zanavyeska

рассказ в
картинках
rasskaz v karteenakh

термометр
tyermomyetr

кукла
kookla

часы
chasy

30

шкафчик
shkafcheek

лекарство
lyekarstva

комнатные туфли
komnatny-ye toofly

пижама
peezhama

шприц
shpreets

микстура
meekstoora

ночная рубашка
nochnaya roobashka

шкаф
shkaf

телевизор
tyelyeveezar

кровать
kravat

диаграмма
deeagramma

гипс
geeps

бинт
beent

синяк
seenyak

кресло на колёсах
kryeslo na kalyesakh

составная картинка-загадка
sastavnaya`karteenka-zagadka

врач
vrach

31

вечеринка
vyechyereenka

воздушные шарики
vazdooshny-ye shareekee

бенгальские огни
byengalskeeye ognee

бумажные шляпки
boomazhny-ye shlyapkee

сладкое
sladkaye

бутерброд
bootyerbrod

луна
loona

конфеты
kanfyety

бисквиты
beeskveety

скатерть
skatyert

пластинки
plasteenkee

торт
tort

шоколад
shakalad

сдобная булочка с изюмом
sdobnaya boolachka s eezyoomam

фонарик
fanareek

игрушки
eegrooshkee

лента
lyenta

свечки
svyechkee

соломинки
salomeenkee

звёзды
zvyosdy

пакеты
pakyety

пудинг
poodeeng

маскарадный костюм
maskaradny kastyoom

подарки
padarkee

окно
akno

желе
zhyelyey

фейерверк
fyeyeryerk

бумажная цепь
boomazhnaya tsyep

33

банан
banan

грейпфрут
gryeypfroot

салат
salat

виноград
veenagrad

цветная
капуста
tsvyetnaya kapoosta

яблоко
yablaka

морковь
markov

лук-порей
look-paryey

тыква
tykva

огурец
agooryets

лимон
leemony

сельдерей
syeldyeryey

фасоль
fasol

вишня
veeshnya

абрикосы
abreekosy

капуста
kapoosta

дыня
dynya

34

магазин
magazeen

сыр
syr

МЯСО
myasa

фрукты
frookty

фрукты
frookty

ОВОЩИ
ovashchee

грибы
greeby

помидоры
pameedory

горох
garokh

сливы
sleevy

малина
maleena

лук
look

персики
pyerseekee

ананас
ananas

картофель
kartofyel

шпинат
shpeenat

рыба
ryba

бакалея
bakalyeya

хлеб
khlyeb

консервы
kansyervy

хлеб
khlyeb

масло
masla

сыр
syr

курица
kooreetsa

яйца
yaytsa

рыба
ryba

мука
mookah

банки
bankee

мясо
myaso

сосиски
saseeskee

кефир
tyefeer

корзина
karzeena

бутылки
bootylkee

брюссельская
капуста
bryoosyelskaya
kapoosta

клубника
kloobneeka

апельсины
apyelseeny

сумки
soomkee

касса
kassa

весы
vyesy

деньги
dyengee

кошелёк
kashyelyok

тележка
для покупок
tyelyezhka dlya pakoopak

сумочка
soomachka

35

пища
peeshcha

завтрак
zavtrak

обед
abyed

кофе
kofye

курица
kooreetsa

варенье
varyenye

мёд
myod

яичница глазунья
yaeechneetsa glazoonya

молоко
malako

сливки
sleevkee

горячий шоколад
garyachee shakalad

отбивные
atbeevny-ye

пиво
peeva

ветчина
vyetcheena

соль
sol

перец
pyeryets

ужин
oozheen

чай
chay

фруктовый сок
frooktovy sok

орехи
aryekhee

мясо
myasa

сахар
sakhar

суп
soop

омлет
amlyet

салат
salat

тушёное мясо
tooshyenoye myasa

блины
bleeny

булочки
boolachkee

рис
rees

вино
veeno

спагетти
spagyettee

соус
so-oos

37

волосы
volasy

бровь
brov

глаз
glaz

нос
nos

щёка
shchyotka

рот
rot

губы
gooby

зубы
zooby

язык
yazyk

подбородок
padbarodak

шея
shyeya

уши
ooshee

голова
galava

лицо
leetso

плечи
plyechee

руки
rookee

локоть
lokat

ладони
ladonee

пальцы
paltsy

большие пальцы
balsheeye palyets

спина
speena

попа
popa

грудь
grood

животик
zheevoteek

колени
kalyenee

ноги
nogee

ноги
nogee

пальцы на ноге
paltsy na nogye

пятка
pyatka

моя одежда
maya adyezhda

трусы
troosy

майка
mayka

брюки
bryookee

джинсы
jeenzy

сорочка
sarochka

юбка
yoobka

рубашка
roobashka

галстук
galstook

шорты
shorty

носки
naskee

свитер
sveetyer

джемпер
jyempyer

кофточка
koftachka

колготы
kalgoty

блузка
bloozka

платье
platye

проссовки
krassofkee

туфли
tooflee

сандалии
sandalee

сапоги
sapagee

перчатки
pyerchatkee

пиджак
peedzhak

куртка
koortka

пальто
palto

носовой платок
nasavoy platok

фуражка
foorazhka

шляпа
shlyapa

пояс
poyas

пуговицы
poogaveetsy

петли
pyetlee

карманы
karmany

застёжка-молния
zastyozhka-molneeya

пряжка
pryazhka

шнурки
shnoorkee

шарф
sharf

39

ЛЮДИ
lyoodee

актёр
aktyor

шеф-повар
shyef-pavar

балерина
balyereena

аквалангист
akvalangeest

космонавт
kasmanavt

дирижёр
deereezhyor

столяр
stalyar

клоун
klo-oon

продавец
pradavyets

солдат
saldat

полицейский
paleetsyeyskee

фермер
fyermyer

певица
pyeveetsa

гонщик
gonshcheek

механик
mayhaneek

художник
khoodozhneek

40

мясник
myasneek

пожарный
pazharny

почтальон
pachtalyon

водолаз
vadalaz

маляр
malyar

машинист
masheeneest

альпинист
alpeeneest

судья
soodya

зубной врач
zoobnoy vrach

работник зоопарка
rabotneek za-aparka

пилот
peelot

пекарь
pyekar

семьи
syemee

| **отец** atyets | **мать** mat | **дочь** doch | **сын** syn | **тётя** tyotya | **дядя** dyadya | **двоюродный брат** dvayoorodny brat | **бабушка** babooshka | **дедушка** dyedooshka |
| **муж** moozh | **жена** zhyena | **сестра** syestra | **брат** brat | | | | | |

41

простые действия

prasty-ye dyeystveeya

улыбаться
oolybatsa

носить
naseet

купаться
koopatsa

думать
doomat

писать
peesat

ползать
polzat

строить
straeet

рубить
roobeet

писать картину
peesat karteenoo

разбить
razbeet

читать
cheetat

чистить
cheesteet

слушать
slooshat

косить
kaseet

падать
padat

мыть
myt

прятаться
pryatatsa

пить
peet

плакать
plakat

смеяться
smyeyatsa

подметать
padmyetat

танцевать
tantsyevat

ловить
laveet

вязать
vyazat

сидеть
seedyet

42

влезать
vlyezat

дуть
doot

играть
eegrat

готовить пищу
gatoveet peeshchoo

драться
dratsa

спать
spat

скакать
skakat

собирать
sabeerat

кидать
keedat

говорить
gavareet

ждать
zhdat

смотреть
smatryet

брать
brat

есть
yest

шить
sheet

тянуть
tyanoot

копать
kapat

петь
pyet

победить
pabyedeet

бегать
byezhat

прыгать
prygat

делать
dyelat

толкать
talkat

стоять
stayat

покупать
pakoopat

ходить
khadeet

43

АНТОНИМЫ
antaneemy

маленький
malyenkee

большой
balshoy

толстый
tolsty

худой
khoodoy

хороший
kharoshee

плохой
plakhoy

половина
palaveena

целый
tsyely

холодный
khalodny

горячий
garyachee

верхний
vyerkhnee

нижний
neezhnee

мягкий
myakhkee

жёсткий
zhyostkee

первый
pyervy

последний
paslyedny

далеко
dalyeko

несколько
nyeskolka

много
mnoga

близко
bleezka

пустой
poostoy

полный
polny

грязный
gryazny

чистый
cheesty

левый
lyevy

высокий
vysokee

низкий
neezkee

медленно
myedlyenna

быстро
bystra

легко
lyekhko

трудно
troodna

длинный
dleenny

короткий
karotkee

вкусно
vkoosna

невкусно
nyefkoosna

наверху
navyerkhoo

внизу
vneezoo

над
nad

под
pod

передняя часть
pyeryednyava chast

задняя часть
zadnyaya chast

мокрый
mokry

сухой
sookhoy

живой
zheevoy

мёртвый
myortvy

темно
tyemno

светло
svyetlo

открытый
atkryty

закрытый
zakryty

поворот
pavarot

правый
pravy

старый
stary

новый
novy

снаружи
snaroosna

внутри
vnootree

Слова употребляемые в сказках

slava oopatryeblyaymy-ye v skazkakh

замок
zamak

дракон
drakon

рыцарь
rytsar

метла
myetla

ведьма
vyedma

пистолет
peestalyet

великан
vyeleekan

пушка
pooshka

пират
peerat

сокровище
sakroveeshchye

волшебная палочка
valshyebnaya palachka

фея
fyeya

волшебный колодец
valshyebny kaladyets

поганка
paganka

эльф
elf

карлик
karleek

фокусник
fokoosneek

разбойник
razboyneek

пустыня
poostynya

индеец
eendyeyets

шериф
shyereef

ковбой
kavboy

почтовая карета
pachtovaya karyeta

46

дьявол
dyavol

корона
karona

дворец
dvaryets

паж
pazh

принцесса
preentsyessa

сабля
sablya

королева
karalyeva

король
karol

принц
preents

ангел
angyel

тюрьма
tyoorma

динозавр
deenazavr

олень
alyen

сани
sanee

дед мороз
dyed maroz

волшебник
valshyebneek

призрак
preezrak

жених
zhyeneekh

невеста
nyevyesta

подружки невести
padroozhkee nyevyestee

чудовище
choodoveeshchye

47

любимые животные
lyoobeemy-ye zheevotny-ye

кошка
koshka

собака
sabaka

кролики
kroleekee

золотые рыбки
zalaty-ye rybkee

ящерицы
yashchyereetsy

попугай
papoogay

лягушки
lyagooshkee

ёж
yozh

тутовый шелкопряд
tootavy shyelkaprygd

попугайчики
papoogaycheekee

ХОМЯК
khamyak

жабы
zhaby

щенки
shchyonkee

голуби
goloobee

мыши
myshee

змеи
zmyey

котята
katyaya

черепахи
chyeryepakhee

48

погода
pagoda

туман
tooman

дождь
dozhd

мороз
maroz

облака
ablaka

снег
snyeg

солнце
solntsye

радуга
radooga

молния
molneeya

роса
rasa

ветер
vyetyer

лёгкий туман
lyokhkee tooman

времена года
vryemyena goda

весна
vyesna

лето
lyeta

осень
osyen

зима
zeema

49

ВИДЫ СПОРТА
veedy sporta

бокс
boks

велосипедный спорт
vyelaseepyedny sport

бейсбол
byeysbol

плавание
plavaneeye

футбол
footbol

гимнастика
geemnasteeka

прыжок в высоту
pryzhok v vysatoo

лыжный спорт
lyzhny sport

автомобильный спорт
avtamabeelny sport

теннис
tyennees

скачки
skachkee

кататься на коньках
katatsya na konkakh

стрельба
stryelba

крикет
kreekyet

тяжёлая атлетика
tyazhyolaya atlyeteeka

скачки с барьерами
skachkee s baryeramee

гоночный трек
ganochny tryek

кататься верхом
katatsya vyerkhom

идти под парусами
eedtee pad paroosamee

настольный теннис
nastolny tyennees

гребля
greblya

борьба
barba

баскетбол
baskyetbol

дзюдо
dzyoodo

цвета
tsvyeta

чёрный
chyorny

оранжевый
aranzhyevy

зелёный
zyelyony

красный
krasny

розовый
rozavy

синий
seenee

белый
byely

коричневый
kareechnyevy

серый
syery

пурпурный
poopoorny

жёлтый
zhyolty

формы
formy

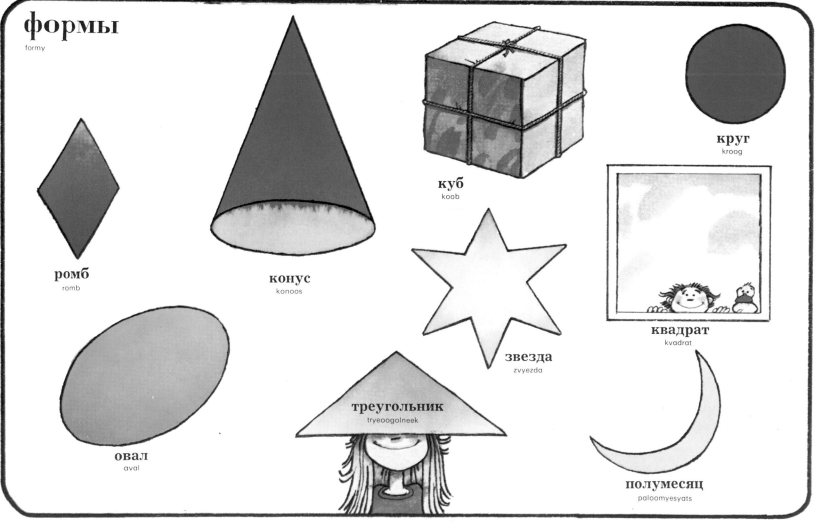

ромб
romb

конус
konoos

куб
koob

круг
kroog

звезда
zvyezda

квадрат
kvadrat

овал
aval

треугольник
tryeoogolneek

полумесяц
paloomyesyats

числа

cheesla

1 **один**
adeen

2 **два**
dva

3 **три**
tree

4 **четыре**
chyetyrye

5 **пять**
pyat

6 **шесть**
shyest

7 **семь**
syem

8 **восемь**
vosyem

9 **девять**
dyevyat

10 **десять**
dyesyat

11 **одиннадцать**
adeennatsat

12 **двенадцать**
dvyenatsat

13 **тринадцать**
treenatsat

14 **четырнадцать**
chyetyrnatsat

15 **пятнадцать**
pyatnatsat

16 **шестнадцать**
shyestnatsat

17 **семнадцать**
syemnatsat

18 **восемнадцать**
vosyemnatsat

19 **девятнадцать**
dyevyatnatsat

20 **двадцать**
dvatsat

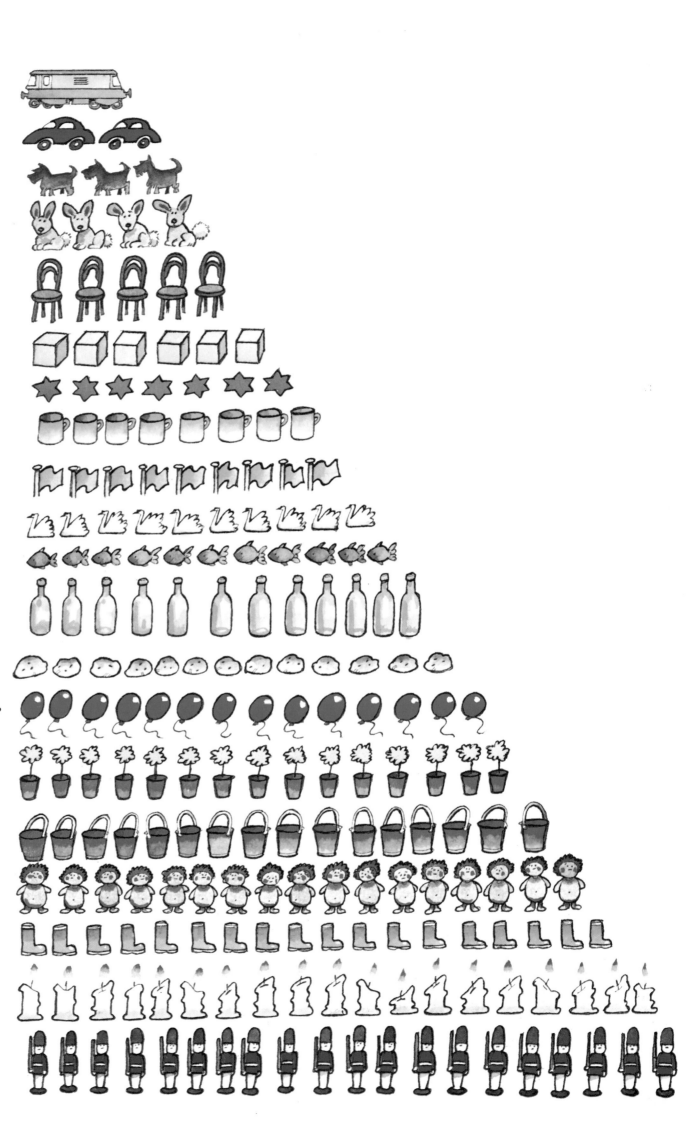

ярмарка
yarmarka

карусель
karoosyel

мат
mat

спираль
speeral

чёртово колесо
chyortava kalyesa

электрические машинки
elyektreechyeskeeye masheenkee

американская горька
amyereekanskaya gorka

набрось-кольцо
nabros-kaltso

воздушная кукуруза
vazdooshnaya kookoorooza

сладкая вата
sladkaya vata

поезд призраков
poyezd preezrakov

тир
teer

цирк
tseerk

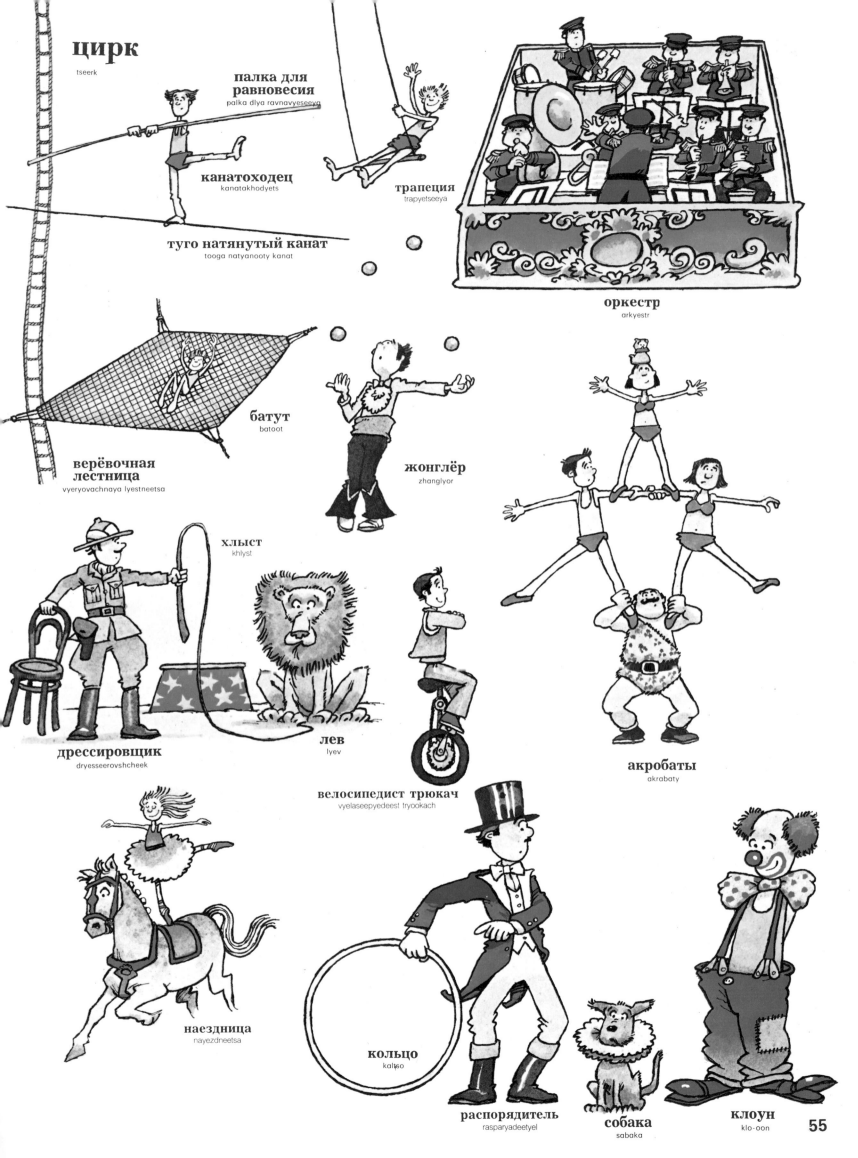

палка для равновесия
palka dlya ravnavyeseeya

канатоходец
kanatakhodyets

трапеция
trapyetseeya

туго натянутый канат
tooga natyanooty kanat

оркестр
arkyestr

батут
batoot

верёвочная лестница
vyeryovachnaya lyestneetsa

жонглёр
zhanglyor

хлыст
khlyst

дрессировщик
dryesseerovshcheek

лев
lyev

велосипедист трюкач
vyelaseepyedeest tryookach

акробаты
akrabaty

наездница
nayezdneetsa

кольцо
kaltso

распорядитель
rasparyadeetyel

собака
sabaka

клоун
klo-oon

55

Saying the words

On this page is the Cyrillic alphabet, with the capital letters and small letters, and the equivalent sounds in English. But some sounds in Russian are quite different from any sounds in English. There is one letter, called a "soft sound" which has no sound of its own but which softens the sound of the letter in front of it. A soft sound often comes after a consonant and makes that consonant sound as if it were followed by a very short y (as in **yet**). The **ы** is a very funny sound and you have to listen to a Russian person saying it before you can pronounce it really correctly yourself.

Below is the start of the alphabetical list of all the words in the pictures in this book. The Russian word, in the Cyrillic alphabet, comes first, then there is its equivalent in the Roman alphabet (this is to help you pronounce the word), followed by the English translation.

А а	a	as in father
Б б	b	as in book
В в	v	as in vine
Г г	g	as in good
Д д	d	as in date
Е е	ye	as in yes
Ё ё	yo	as in yonder
Ж ж	s	as in pleasure
З з	z	as in zoo
И и	ee	as in meet
Й й	y	as in boy
К к	k	as in kind

Л л	l	as in lamb
М м	m	as in mother
Н н	n	as in noose
О о	o	as in pot
П п	p	as in pen
Р р	r	as in read
С с	s	as in sun
Т т	t	as in tar
У у	oo	as in fool
Ф ф	f	as in funny
Х х	ch	as in loch
Ц ц	tz	as in quartz

Ч ч	ch	as in chain
Ш ш	sh	as in sheep
Щ щ	shch	as in fresh cheese
Ъ ъ		this gives a consonant a hard sound
Ы ы	i	as in rip
Ь ь		this gives a consonant a soft sound
Э э	e	as in best
Ю ю	you	as in youth
Я я	ya	as in yard

Index   Words in the pictures

блузка	bloozka	blouse
блюдца	blyoodtsya	saucers
бобр	bobr	beaver
бокс	boks	boxing
болты	bolty	bolts
большой	balshoy	big
большой палец	balshoy palyets	thumb
бороться	barotsa	fight
борьба	barba	wrestling
бочка	bochka	barrel
брат	brat	brother
брать	brat	take
брикет	breekyet	straw bales
бровь	brof	eyebrow
брюки	bryookee	trousers
брюссельская капуста	bryoossyelskaya kapoosta	brussel sprout
буйвол	booyvol	buffalo
булочки	boolochkee	rolls
бумага	boomaga	paper
бумажная цепь	boomazhnaya tsyep	paper chain
бумажные шляпки	boomazhnye shlyapkee	paper hats
бусы	boosy	beads
бутерброд	bootyerbrod	sandwich
бутылка	bootylka	bottle
буфер	boofyer	buffer
бык	byk	bull
быстро	bystra	fast
вагон-ресторан	vagon-ryestoran	buffet car
вагоны	vagony	carriages
ванна	vanna	bath
ванная	vannaya	bathroom
варенье	varyenye	jam
вата	vata	cotton wool
ведро	vyedro	bucket
ведьма	vyedma	witch
великан	vyeleekan	giant
велосипед	vyelaseepyed	bicycle
велосипедист трюкач	vyelaseepyedeest tryookach	trick cyclist
велосипедный спорт	vyelaseepyedny sport	cycle riding
верблюд	vyerblyood	camel
верёвка	vyeryofka	rope
верёвочная лестница	vyeryovochnaya lyestneetsa	rope ladder
верстак	vyerstak	work bench
вертолёт	vertalyot	helicopter
верхний	vyerkhnee	top
весло	vyeslo	paddle
весна	vyesna	spring
весы	vyesy	scales
ветряная мельница	vyetryanaya myelneetsa	windmill
ветчина	vyetcheena	ham
вечеринка	vyechyereenka	party
вешалка	vyeshalka	peg
взлётнопосадочная полоса	vzlyotnapasadachnaya palosa	runway
виды спорта	veedy sporta	sports
вилки	veelkee	forks (table)
вилы	veely	forks (garden)
вино	veeno	wine
виноград	veenagrad	grape
вишня	veeshnya	cherry taste
влезать	vlyezat	climb
внизу	vneezoo	downstairs
внутри	vnootree	inside
вода	vada	water
водитель	vadeetyel	driver
водно-лыжник	vodna-lyzhneek	water skier
водолаз в глубокие воды	vadalaz v glooboekeeye vady	deep sea diver
воздушная кукуруза	vazdooshnaya kookoorooza	popcorn
воздушный змей	vozdooshnye zmyey	kite
воздушный шар	vazdooshny shar	balloon
вокзал	vakzal	station
волк	volk	wolf
волны	volny	waves
волосы	volasy	hair
волшебная палочка	valshebnaya palochka	wand
волшебник	valshyebneek	wizard
волшебный колодец	valshyebny kaladyets	wishing well
врач	vrach	doctor
времена года	vryemyena goda	seasons
высокий	vysokee	high
вязать	vyazat	knit
гавань	gavan	harbour
гадко	gadka	nasty
гаечный ключ	gayechny klyooch	spanner
газета	gazyeta	newspaper
газонокосилка	gazanakaseelka	lawn mower
гайка	gayka	nut
галстук	galstook	tie
галька	galka	pebble
гараж	garazh	garage
гармошка	garmoshka	mouth organ
гвозди	gvozdee	nails
гвоздик с широкой шляпкой	gvozdeek s sheerokoy shlyapkoy	tack
гимнастика	geemnasteeka	gymnastics
гиппопотам	geepapatam	hippopotamus
гипс	geeps	plaster
гитара	geetara	guitar
гладильная доска	gladeelnaya daska	ironing board
глаз	glaz	eye
глобус	globoos	globe
говорить	gavareet	talk
голова	galava	head
головастики	galavasteekee	tadpoles
голуби	galoobee	pigeons
голубь	galoob	pigeon
гоночная машина	ganochnaya masheena	racing car
гоночный трек	ganochny tryek	speedway racing
гонщик	gonshcheek	racing car driver
горилла	gareella	gorilla
горка для катания	gorka dlya kataneeya	slide
горох	garokh	pea
горы	gory	mountains
горячий	garyachee	hot
горячий шоколад	garyachee shakalad	hot chocolate
гостиная	gasteenaya	living room
гостиница	gasteeneetsa	hotel
готовить пищу	gatoveet peeshchoo	cook
грабли	grablee	rake
гребля	greblya	rowing
гребная лодка	gryebnaya lodka	rowing boat
грейпфрут	gryeypfroot	grapefruit
грибы	greeby	mushrooms
грудь	grood	chest (body)
грузовик	groozaveek	lorry
грязный	gryazny	dirty
грязь	gryaz	mud

губка	goobka	sponge
губы	gooby	lips
гусеница	goosyeneetsa	caterpillar
гуси	goosee	geese
гусята	goosta	goslings
далеко	dalyeko	far
дверь	dver	door
дворец	dvaryets	palace
двоюродный брат	dvayoorodny brat	cousin (man)
девочки	dyevochkee	girls
дед мороз	dyed maroz	Father Christmas
дедушка	dyedooshka	grandfather
делать	dyelat	to make
дельфин	dyelfeen	dolphin
деньги	dyengee	money
деревня	dyeryevnya	countryside
дерево	dyeryeva	tree
деревья	dyryevya	trees
деревянный брусок	dyeryevyanny broosok	wood
дети	dyetee	children
детская коляска	dyetskaya kalyaska	pram
детская складная коляска	dyetskaya skladnaya kolyaska	push chair
детские качели	dyetskeeye kachelee	seesaw
джемпер	jyempyer	jumper
джинсы	jeenzy	jeans
диаграмма	deeagramma	chart
динозавр	deenazavr	dinosaur
дирижёр	deereezhyor	conductor
длинный	dleenny	long
дождь	dozhd	rain
дом	dom	house
дорога	daroga	road
доска	daska	plank, blackboard
дочь	doch	daughter
дракон	drakon	dragon
драться	dratsa	fight
дрель	dryel	drill
дрова	drava	firewood
думать	doomat	to think
дуть	doot	to blow
душ	doosh	shower
дым	dym	smoke
дыня	dynya	melon
дьявол	dyavol	devil
дядя	dyadya	uncle
есть	yest	eat
ёж	yozh	hedgehog
жабы	zhaby	toads
жалюзи	zhalyoozy	blinds
ждать	zhdat	wait
желе	zhyelye	jelly
железная дорога	zhylyeznaya daroga	train set
жена	zhyena	wife
жених	zhyeneekh	bridegroom
женщина	zhyenshcheena	woman
жёлтый	zhyolty	yellow
жёсткий	zhyostkee	hard
живая изгородь	zheevaya eezgarad	hedge
живой	zheevoy	alive
живопись	zheevapees	painting
животик	zheevoteek	tummy
жилой дом	zheeloy dom	flats
жилойдом на ферме	zheeloydom na fyermye	farmhouse
жираф	zheeraf	giraffe
забор	zabor	fence
завтрак	zavtrak	breakfast
задняя часть	zadnyaya chast	back
закрытый	zakryty	closed
замок	zamok	castle
занавеска	zanavyeska	curtain
застёжка-молния	zastyozhka-molneeya	zip
звёзды	zvyozdy	stars
зебра	zyebra	zebra
зелёный	zyelyony	green
земля	zyemlya	earth
зеркало	zyerkalo	mirror
зерно	zyerno	corn
зима	zeema	winter
змей	zmyey	snake
значок	znachok	badge
золотые рыбки	zalatye rybkee	goldfish
зонт	zont	umbrella
зоопарк	zaapark	zoo
зубная паста	zoobnaya pasta	toothpaste
зубная щётка	zoobnaya shchyotka	toothbrush
зубной врач	zoobnoy vrach	dentist
зубы	zooby	teeth
игральные кости	eegralny-ye kostee	dice
играть	eegrat	to play
игрушки	eegrooshkee	toys
идти под парусами	eedtee pad paroosamee	sailing
индеец	eendyeyets	Indian
индюки	eendyookee	turkeys
календарь	kalyendar	calendar
калитка	kaleetka	gate
камни	kamnee	stones
канал	kanal	canal
канатоходец	kanatakhodyets	tight rope walker
канцелярские кнопки	kantsyelyarskeeye knopkee	drawing pins
капот	kapot	bonnet (of car)
капуста	kapoosta	cabbage
карандаши	karandashee	pencils
карлик	karleek	dwarf (man)
карманы	karmany	pockets
карта	karta	map
картины	karteeny	pictures
картофель	kartofyel	potato
карты	karty	cards
карусель	karoosyel	roundabout
касса	kassa	cash desk
кастелянт	kastyelyant	porter
кастрюли	kastryoolee	saucepans
каталка	katalka	trolley
кататься верхом	katatsa vyerkhom	riding
кататься на коньках	katatsa na konkakh	skating
каток	katok	roller
кафе	kafye	café
кафельная плитка	kafyelnaya pleetka	tile
качели	kachyelee	swings
квадрат	kvadrat	square
кельма	kyelma	trowel
кенгуру	kyengooroo	kangaroo
кидать	keedat	to throw
кинотеатр	keenatyeatr	cinema
кирпичи	keerpeechee	bricks
кисти	keestee	brushes

кит	keet	whale		куст	koost	bush
клей	klyey	glue		кухня	kookhnya	kitchen
клоун	klo-oon	clown				
клубника	kloobneeka	strawberry		ладони	ladonee	palms (hands)
клумба	kloomba	flower bed		лампа	lampa	lamp
ключ	klyooch	key		лампа	lampa	bulb
книги	kneegee	books		ласты	lasty	flippers
книжный шкаф	kneezhny shkaf	bookshelf		лебеди	lyebyedee	swans
ковбой	kavboy	cowboy		лев	lev	lion
ковёр	kavyor	carpet		левый	levy	left
коврик	kovreek	rug		легко	lekh ko	easy
козёл	kazyol	goat		лекарство	lyekarstva	medicine
колготы	kalgoty	tights		лента	lyenta	ribbon
колени	kalyenee	knees		леопард	lyeopard	leopard
колесо	kalyeso	wheel		лес	lyec	forest
колокольчик	kalakolcheek	hand bell		лестница	lyectneetsa	stairs, ladder
комнатные	komnatny-ye			лето	lyeto	summer
туфли	toofly	slippers		летучая мышь	lyetoochaya mysh	bat
комод	kamod	chest		лёгкий туман	lyokhkee tooman	mist
кондуктор	kandooktor	guard		лимоны	leemony	lemons
консервы	kansyervy	tins		линейка	leenyeyka	ruler
конус	kanoos	cone		лиса	leesa	fox
конфеты	kanfyety	sweets		листья	leestya	leaves
копать	kapat	to dig		лисята	leesyata	fox cubs
копилка	kapeelka	money box		лифт	leeft	lift
корабль	karabl	ship		лицо	leetso	face
корзина	karzeena	basket		ловить	laveet	catch
корзина для	karzeena dlya	wastepaper		ложки	lozhkee	spoons
бумаг	boomag	bin		локомотив	lakamateev	engine
коричневый	kareechnyevy	brown		локоть	lokot	elbow
коробки	karobkee	boxes		лопата	lapata	spade
корова	karova	cow		лопатка	lapatka	spade, small
коровник	karovneek	cowshed		лоск	losk	polish
королева	karalyeva	queen		лошадь	loshad	horse
король	karol	king		лошадь качалка	loshad kachalka	rocking horse
корона	karona	crown		лужа	loozha	puddle
короткий	karotkee	short		лук	look	onion
косить	kaseet	to cut		лук-порей	look-paryey	leek
космонавты	kasmanavty	astronauts		лук и стрела	look ee stryela	bow & arrow
костёр	kastyor	bonfire		луна	loona	moon
костыли	kastylee	crutches		лыжный спорт	lyzhny sport	skiing
кость	kost	bone		львята	lvyata	lion cubs
котята	katyata	kittens		любимые	lyoobeemy-ye	
кофе	kofye	coffee		животные	zheevotny-ye	pets
кофточка	koftachka	cardigan		люди	lyoodee	people
кошелёк	kashyelyok	purse		лягушки	lyagooshkee	frogs
кошка	koshka	cat				
краб	krab	crab		магазин	magazeen	shop
кран	kran	crane, tap		магазин игрушек	magazeen	toy shop
краски	kraskee	paints			eegrooshyek	
красный	krasny	red		майка	mayka	vest
кресло	kryeslo	chair		мальчики	malcheekee	boys
кресло на колёсах	kalyosakna kryeslo	wheelchair		маляр	malyar	painter
крикет	kreekyet	cricket		маленький	malyenkee	small
кровать	kravat	bed		малина	maleena	raspberry
крокодил	krakadeel	crocodile		марионетки	maree-anyetkee	puppets
кролики	kroleekee	rabbits		маскарадный	maskaradny	fancy dress
кроссовки	krassofkee	gymshoes		костюм	kastyoom	
крот	krot	mole		маски	maskee	masks
круг	kroog	circle		маслёнка	maslyonka	oil can
крыло	krylo	wing		масло	maslo	butter, oil
крыша	krysha	roof		мастерская	mastyerskaya	workshop
куб	koob	cube		мат	mat	mat
кубики	koobeekee	blocks		мать	mat	mother
кукла	kookla	doll		машина	masheena	car
куклы	kookly	dolls		машинист	masheeneest	engine driver
кукольный дом	kookalny dom	dolls' house		маяк	mayak	lighthouse
купальный	koonalny	swimsuit		медведь	myevyed	bear
костюм	kastyoom			медвежонок	myedvyezhonok	teddy bear
купаться	koopatsa	to bath		медленно	myedlyenna	slowly
курица	kooreetsa	chicken		медсестра	myedsyestra	nurse
куртка	koortka	anorak		мел	myel	chalk
куры	koory	hens		метла	myetla	broom
курятник	kooryatneek	hen house		метла	myetla	broomstick

механик	*mayhaneek*	mechanic
мерная лента	*myernaya lyenta*	tape measure
мешки	*myeshkee*	sacks
мёд	*myod*	honey
мёртвый	*myortvy*	dead
милицейская машина	*meeleetsyeyskaya masheena*	police car
милиционер	*meeleetsyanyer*	policeman
миски	*myskee*	bowls
мишень	*meeshyeen*	target
много	*mnoga*	many
мойка машин	*moyka masheen*	car wash
мокрый	*mokry*	wet
молния	*molneeya*	lightning
молоко	*malako*	milk
молоток	*malatok*	hammer
мольберт	*malbyert*	easel
море	*morye*	sea
морковь	*markov*	carrot
мороженое	*marozhyenoye*	ice cream
мороз	*maroz*	frost
морская водоросль	*morskaya vadarosl*	sea weed
морская звезда	*morskaya zbyezda*	star fish
морская раковина	*morskaya pakabeena*	sea shell
моряк	*maryak*	sailor
мост	*most*	bridge
мотор	*mator*	engine
моторная лодка	*matornaya lodka*	motor boat
мотоцикл	*matatseekl*	motor cycle
мотыга	*matyga*	hoe
мотылёк	*matylyok*	moth
муж	*moozh*	husband
мужчина	*moozhcheena*	man
мука	*mooka*	flour
муравей	*mooravyey*	ant
мусор	*moosar*	rubbish
мусорный ящик	*moosarny yashcheek*	dustbin
муха	*mookha*	fly
мыло	*mylo*	soap
мыльные пузыри	*mylny-ye poozyree*	bubbles
мыть	*myt*	wash
мыши	*myshee*	mice
мягкий	*myakhkee*	soft
мясник	*myasneek*	butcher
мясо	*myasa*	meat
мяч	*myach*	ball
мячи	*myachee*	balls
наблюдательная башня	*nablyoodatyelna-ya bashnya*	control tower
набор инструментов	*nabor eenstroom-yentov*	toolset
набрось-кольцо	*nabros-kaltso*	hoop-la
наверху	*navyerkhoo*	upstairs
над	*nad*	over
наездница	*nayezdneetsa*	bare-back rider (woman)
наждачная бумага	*nazhdachnaya boomaga*	sandpaper
напильник	*napeelneek*	file
насос	*nasos*	air pump
настольный теннис	*nastolny tyennees*	table tennis
невеста	*nyevyesta*	bride
невкусно	*nyefkoosna*	nasty taste
несколько	*nyeskoylko*	a few
нижний	*neezhny*	bottom
низкий	*neezkee*	low
новый	*novy*	new
ноги	*nogee*	feet & legs

ножи	*nozhee*	knives
ножницы	*nozhneetsy*	scissors
нос	*nos*	nose
носить	*naseet*	carry
носки	*naskee*	socks
носовой платок	*nasovoy platok*	handkerchief
носорог	*nasarog*	rhinoceros
ночная рубашка	*nochnaya roobashka*	nightdress
обед	*abyed*	lunch or dinner
обед в походе	*abyed f pakhodye zaftrak*	picnic
завтрак		
обезьяна	*abyezyana*	ape
облака	*oblaka*	clouds
обои	*aboy*	wallpaper
овал	*aval*	oval
овощи	*ovashchee*	vegetables
овцы	*avtsy*	sheep
овчарка	*avcharka*	sheep dog
огурец	*agooryets*	cucumber
одежда	*adyezhda*	clothes
озеро	*ozyera*	lake
окно	*akno*	window
олень	*alyen*	deer
омлет	*amlyet*	omelette
опилки	*appelkee*	sawdust
оранжевый	*aranzhyevy*	orange
орехи	*aryekhee*	nuts
орёл	*aryol*	eagle
оса	*asa*	wasp
осень	*osyem*	autumn
осёл	*asyol*	donkey
острова	*astrava*	islands
отбивные	*atbeevny-ye*	chops
отбойный молоток	*atboyny malatok*	drill
отвёртка	*atvyorka*	screwdriver
отец	*atyets*	father
открытый	*atkryty*	open
падать	*padat*	to fall
паж	*pazh*	pageboy
пакеты	*pakyety*	parcels
палатки	*palatkee*	tents
палка для равновесия	*palka dlya ravnavyeseeya*	balancing pole
палки	*palkee*	sticks
пальто	*palto*	coat
пальцы	*paltsy*	fingers
пальцы на ноге	*paltsy na nogye*	toes
памятник	*pamyatneek*	statue
панда	*panda*	panda
парашют	*parashyoot*	parachute
парк	*park*	park
паровозный машинист	*parovozny masheeneest*	train driver
парта	*parta*	desk
парусная лодка	*paroosnaya lodka*	sailing boat
пастух	*pastookh*	shepherd
паук	*paook*	spider
паутина	*payteena*	cobweb
певица	*pyeveetsa*	singer (woman)
пекарь	*pyekar*	baker
пеликан	*pyeleekan*	pelican
первый	*pyervy*	first
передник	*pyeryedneek*	apron
передняя часть	*pyeryednyaya chast*	front
перец	*pyeryets*	pepper
перила	*pyereela*	railings
перочинный ножик	*pyeracheenny nazheek*	pen knife

персики	pyerseekee	peaches
переход	pyeryekhod	crossing
перчатки	pyerchatkee	gloves
перья	pyerya	feathers
песчаный замок	pyeschany zamak	sand castle
песчаный карьер	pyeschany karyer	sandpit
петли	pyetlee	button holes
петух	pyetookh	cockerel
петь	pyet	to sing
пиво	peeva	beer
пиджак	peedzhak	jacket
пижама	peezhama	pyjamas
пила	peela	saw
пилот	peelot	pilot
пингвин	peengveen	penguin
пират	peerat	pirate
писать	peesat	to write
писать картину	peesat karteenoo	to paint
пистолет	peestalyet	pistol
письмо	peesmo	letter
пить	peet	to drink
пишущая машинка	peeshooshchaya masheenka	typewriter
плавание	plavaneeye	swimming
плакать	plakat	to cry
пластилин	plasteeleen	clay
пластинки	plasteenkee	records
платформа	platforma	platform
платье	platye	dress
плечи 38	plyechee	shoulders
плита	pleeta	cooker
плохой	plakhoy	bad
площадка для игр	plashchadka dlya eegr	playground
плуг	ploog	plough
победить	pabyedeet	to win
поводок	pavodak	dog lead
повозка	pavoska	cart
поворот	pavarot	turn
поганка	paganka	toadstool
погода	pagoda	weather
под	pad	under
подарки	padarkee	presents
подбородок	padbarodak	chin
подводная лодка	padvodnaya lodka	submarine
подметать	padmyetat	to sweep
поднос	padnos	tray
подружки невесты	padroozhkee nyevyesty	bridesmaids
подушка	padooshka	pillow, cushion
поезд	poyezd	train
поезд призраков	poyezd preezrakov	ghost train
пожарная машина	pazharnaya masheena	fire engine
пожарный	pazharny	fireman
покупать	pakoo pat	to buy
полено	polyeno	log
ползать	palzat	to crawl
поле	polye	field
полный	polny	full
половина	palaveena	half
полотенце	palatyentsye	towel
полумесяц	paloomyesyats	crescent
помидоры	pameedory	tomatoes
пони	ponee	pony
поросята	parasyata	piglets
попа	popa	bottom (body)
попугай	papoogay	parrot
последний	paslyednee	last
постель	pastyel	bed
потолок	patalok	ceiling
почтальон	pachtalyon	postman
почтовая карета	pachtovaya karyeta	stage coach
пояс	poyas	belt
правый	pravy	right
призрак	preezrak	ghost
принц	preents	prince
принцесса	preentsyessa	princess
прихожая	preekhozhaya	hall
прицеп	preetsyep	trailer
проводник	pravodneek	ticket collector
продавец	pradavyets	shop keeper(man
проигрыватель	pra-eegry-vatyel	record player
простые действия	prasty-ye dyeystveeye	doing words
простыня	prastynya	sheet
пруд	prood	pond
прыгать	prygat	to jump
прыжок в высоту	pryzhok v vysatoo	high jump
пряжка	pryazhka	buckle
прятаться	pryatatsa	to hide
птицы	pteetsy	birds
птичье гнездо	pteechye gnyezdo	bird's nest
пугало	poogala	scarecrow
пуговицы	poogaveetsy	buttons
пудинг	poodeeng	pudding
пурпурный	poopoorny	purple
пустыня	poostynya	desert
пуховое одеяло	pookhavaye adyeala	eiderdown
пушка	pooshka	cannon
пчела	pchyela	bee
пылесос	pylyesos	vacuum cleaner
пыльная тряпка	pylnaya tryapka	duster
работник зоопарка	rabotneek za-aparka	zookeeper
радио	radeeo	radio
радуга	radooga	rainbow
разбить	razbeet	to break
разбойник	razboyneek	robber
разбрызгиватель	razbryzgeevatyel	sprinkler
ракета	rakyeta	rocket
ракетки	rakyetkee	bats
раковина	rakaveena	sink (kitchen)
распорядитель	rasparyadeetyel	manager
рассада	rassada	plants
рассказ в картинках	rasskaz v karteenakh	comic
расчёска	raschyoska	comb
ребёнок	ryebyonak	baby
резать	ryezat	to cut
резинка	ryezeenka	eraser
река	ryeka	river
рельсы	ryelsy	railway lines
речка	ryechka	stream
рис	rees	rice
рисунок	reesoonak	drawing
рисунок	reesoonak	painting
робот	rabot	robot
рога	raga	horns
розетка	razyetka	switch
розовый	rozavy	pink
ролики	roleekee	roller skates
ромб	romb	diamond
роса	rasa	dew
рот	rot	mouth
рояль	rayal	piano
рубанок	roobanak	plane
рубашка	roobashka	shirt
рубить	roobeet	to chop
ружьё	roozhyo	gun

руки	rookee	arms & hands
рулетка	roolyetka	tape measure
ручка	roochka	door handle
ручки	roochkee	pens
рыба	ryba	fish
рыбак	rybak	fisherman
рыбачья лодка	rybachya lodka	fishing boat
рынок	rynak	market
рыцарь	rytsar	knight
сабля	sablya	sword
салат	salat	salad
самокат	samakat	scooter
самолёт	samalyot	aeroplane
сандалии	sandalee	sandals
сани	sanee	sleigh
сапоги	sapagee	boots
сарайчик	saraycheek	shed, hut
сахар	sakhar	sugar
светло	svyetlo	light
светофор	svyetafor	traffic lights
свечки	svyechkee	candles
свинарник	sveenarneek	pigsty
свиньи	sveenee	pigs
свисток	sveestok	whistle
свитер	sveetyer	sweater
сдобная булочка с изюмом	sdobnaya boolachka s eezyoomam	bun
седло	syedla	saddle
сельдерей	syeldyeryey	celery
семафор	syemafor	train signal
семена	syemyena	seeds
семьи	syemee	families
сено	syeno	hay
сестра	syestra	sister
сеть	syet	net
серый	syery	grey
сидеть	seedyet	to sit
синий	seenee	blue
синяк	seenyak	black eye
скакалка	skakalka	skipping rope
скакать	skakat	skip
скалы	skaly	rocks
скамейка	skamyeyka	bench
скатерть	skatyert	table cloth
скачки	skachkee	horse racing
скачки с барьерами	skachkee s baryeramee	show jumping
сковорода	skavaroda	frying pan
скорая помощь	skoraya pomashch	ambulance
сладкая вата	sladkaya vata	candy floss
сладкое	sladkoye	dessert
сливки	sleevkee	cream
сливы	sleevy	plums
слова употребляемые в сказках	slava oopatryeblyaymy-ye v skzkakh	storybook words
слон	slon	elephant
слушать	slooshat	to listen
смеяться	smyeyatsa	to laugh
смотреть	smatryet	to watch
снаружи	snaroozhee	out
снег	snyeg	snow
собака	sabaka	dog
собирать	sabeerat	to pick
сова	sava	owl
совок для мусора	savok dlya moosara	dustpan
сокровище	sakroveeshchye	treasure
солдатики	saldateekee	toy soldiers
солнце	solntsye	sun
соломенная шляпа	salamyenaya shlyapa	straw hat
соломинки	salomeenkee	straws
соль	sol	salt
сорочка	sarochka	t-shirt
сосиски	saseeskee	sausages
составная картинка-загадка	sastavnaya karteenka-zagadka	jigsaw
соус	so-oos	sauce
спагетти	spagyettee	spaghetti
спальня	spalnya	bedroom
спать	spat	to sleep
спираль	speeral	helter skelter
спички	speechkee	matches
стакан	stakan	glass
стаканы	stakany	glasses
старый	stary	old
стена	styena	wall
стиральная машина	steeralnaya masheena	washing machine
стиральный порошок	steeralny parashok	washing powder
стог сена	stog syena	hay stack
стол	stol	table
столяр	stolyar	carpenter
сточный жёлоб	stochny zhyolab	gutter
стоять	stayat	stand
страус	straoos	ostrich
стрельба	stryelba	shooting
строить	straeet	to build
стружки	stroozhkee	shavings
ступеньки	stoopyenkee	steps
стюардесса	styooardyessa	air hostess
судья	soodya	judge
сумки	soomkee	bags
сумочка	soomachka	handbag
сухой	sookhoy	dry
сын	syn	son
сыр	syr	cheese
таблетки	tablyetkee	pills
табуретка	tabooryetka	stool
такси	taksee	taxi
танк	tank	tank
танкер	tankyer	oil tanker
танцевать	tantsyevat	to dance
тарелки	taryelkee	plates
тачка	tachka	wheelbarrow
телевизор	tyelyeveezor	television
тележка для покупок	tyelyezhka dlya pakoopak	trolley
телефон	tyelyefon	telephone
телёнок	tyelyonak	calf
темно	tyemno	dark
теннис	tyennees	tennis
теплица	tyepleetsa	greenhouse
термометр	tyermomyetr	thermometer
тётя	tyotya	aunt
тигр	teegr	tiger
тир	teer	rifle range
тиски	teeskee	vice
товарный поезд	tavarny poyezd	goods train
толкать	talkat	to push
толстый	toltsy	fat
топор	tapor	axe
торт	tort	cake
трава	trava	grass
трактор	traktar	tractor
трапеция	trapyetseeya	trapeze
треугольник	tryeoogolneek	triangle
тропинка	trapeenka	path
тротуар	tratooar	pavement
труба	trooba	pipe, chimney, trumpet
трудно	troodna	difficult
трусы	troosy	pants
туго натянутый канат	tooga natyanooty kanat	tightrope
туман	tooman	fog

62